STEVENSON • WATTERS • LEYH • ALLEN • NOWAK • LAIHO

LUMBERJANES™

BAND TOGETHER

BOOM! BOX™

BOOM! BOX™

LUMBERJANES Volume Five, December 2016. Published by BOOM! Box, a division of Boom Entertainment, Inc. Lumberjanes is ™ & © 2016 Shannon Watters, Grace Ellis, Noelle Stevenson & Brooke Allen. Originally published in single magazine form as LUMBERJANES No. 13, 18-20. ™ & © 2015 Shannon Watters, Grace Ellis, Noelle Stevenson & Brooke Allen. All rights reserved. BOOM! Box™ and the BOOM! Box logo are trademarks of Boom Entertainment, Inc., registered in various countries and categories. All characters, events, and institutions depicted herein are fictional. Any similarity between any of the names, characters, persons, events, and/or institutions in this publication to actual names, characters, and persons, whether living or dead, events, and/or institutions is unintended and purely coincidental. BOOM! Box does not read or accept unsolicited submissions of ideas, stories, or artwork.

A catalog record of this book is available from OCLC and from the BOOM! Studios website, www.boom-studios.com, on the Librarians Page.

BOOM! Studios, 5670 Wilshire Boulevard, Suite 450, Los Angeles, CA 90036-5679. Printed in China. First Printing.

ISBN: 978-1-60886-919-0, eISBN: 978-1-61398-590-8

THIS LUMBERJANES FIELD MANUAL BELONGS TO:

NAME:_____

TROOP:_____

DATE INVESTED:_____

FIELD MANUAL TABLE OF CONTENTS

LUMBERJANES
FIELD MANUAL

For the Intermediate Program

Tenth Edition • May 1984

Prepared for the

**Miss Qiunzella Thiskwin
Penniquiqul Thistle Crumpet's
CAMP FOR** HARDCORE LADY-TYPES

"Friendship to the Max!"

A MESSAGE FROM THE LUMBERJANES HIGH COUNCIL

Friendship is amazing. There are many valuable things in life, but friendship may be one of the most important. To live life without the experience of friendship, would be a life that we would not wish upon anyone. Human interaction is a necessity to survival, and when it comes to survival at camp, that could be literal. Developed friendships, friendships that will truly last the ages, are essential to the successful well being of anyone.

The definition of a friend is, "A person whom one knows, likes, and trusts." But to us here with the Lumberjane Scouts, friendship is so much more than that. Our entire camp curriculum is built around the long lasting relationships that we hope every Lumberjane Scout has a chance to build in their time here. We don't need to define friendship based off of actions or words, but by emotional connection that will form naturally as we all learn to work and live together. During your time at camp, we hope that you experience many great things.

We want you to know what it feels like to fall from great heights with the wind surrounding you, and know that you will be caught. You will also have someone waiting for you at the bottom to catch you so that you may be able to make the climb again together. One of our greatest goals for you is to experience freedom, the ability to be yourself and let go of any pressures of the world outside of this camp.

We want you to feel free to be who you truly are, to be the hardcore lady-type, the amazing Lumberjanes that you are on the inside and outside. We look forward to watching you, and your friends, take on the world one day at a time.

THE LUMBERJANES PLEDGE

I solemnly swear to do my best
Every day, and in all that I do,
To be brave and strong,
To be truthful and compassionate,
To be interesting and interested,
To pay attention and question
The world around me,
To think of others first,
To always help and protect my friends,
~~To respect nature and fulfill my duty~~

THEN THERE'S A LINE ABOUT GOD, OR WHATEVER

And to make the world a better place
For Lumberjane scouts
And for everyone else.

LUMBERJANES™

BAND TOGETHER

Chapter 17 Written by
Noelle Stevenson & Shannon Watters

Chapters 18-20 Written by
Shannon Watters & Kat Leyh

Chapter 17 Illustrated by
Brooke Allen

Chapters 18-20 Illustrated by
Carolyn Nowak

Colors by
Maarta Laiho

Letters by
Aubrey Aiese

Cover by
Brooke Allen
with colors by **Maarta Laiho**

Badge Design by
Scott Newman

Designer
Kelsey Dieterich

Associate Editor
Whitney Leopard

Editor
Dafna Pleban

*Special thanks to **Kelsey Pate** for giving the Lumberjanes their name.*

Created by **Shannon Watters, Grace Ellis, Noelle Stevenson & Brooke Allen**

LUMBERJANES FIELD MANUAL

CHAPTER SEVENTEEN

Lumberjanes "Out-of-Doors" Program Field

BEGINNER'S LUCK BADGE

"Everyone Starts Somewhere"

Every story has a beginning, and every race has a start line. You don't finish things halfway, you begin and complete them from start to finish. Nature is a great place to gain experience in the light of the sun but a true Lumberjane knows the importance of learning things from square one. It is at Lumberjanes Camp that our Lumberjanes will be able to learn new skills and lessons throughout their time there. We don't expect every camper to come in with the knowledge already in their heads because one of the joys of this camp is being able to pass on knowledge to your fellow campers.

The *Beginner's Luck* badge is the for Lumberjane who jumps feet first into the unknown. The Lumberjane who is willing to learn as they go through camp, who will take the experiences and lessons of others and apply them in their day-to-day life at camp. The *Beginner's Luck* badge is earned by multiple methods, by either jumping into a course or curriculum without any prior knowledge and using their

already acquired skills to come out with top marks. Or, a Lumberjane is able to earn the *Beginner's Luck* badge through a series of tests that are set up by their counselor. This is not only the most popular way to earn the badge, but often accepted as the most enjoyable since often time the tests will include working together with your cabin, with your friends.

The history of the *Beginner's Luck* badge starts at the beginning of the Lumberjane camp history. It is in fact one of the original badges from that time, just with a better name. Back then, the *Beginner's Luck* badge was often referred to as the *Guppy* badge, but after much deliberation, we find that while we teach a lot of the same lessons in both the badges, the *Beginner's Luck* badge is just a better name. The biggest and most important lesson to keep in mind with this badge is that while everyone has to start at the beginning, you might be able to skip a step or two but you won't be able to know which steps until you start.

I'll take that.

mrrrr...

Aw, you just wanted a friend, didn't you?

We have to take Mr. Sparkles back to his friend, but I'll be your pal.

We're going back to Lumberjanes camp...

...you'll make an awesome scout, I bet...

will co

The
It he
appeara
dress f
Further
Lumber
to have
part in
Thiskv
Hardc
have
them

CHEER UP, JEN!

I'LL BE YOUR PAL.

The
yellow, short sl
emb
the w
choose
slacks,
made o
out-of-d
green bere
the colla
Shoes ma
heels, rou
socks sho
the uniform. Ne
belong with a Lumberjane unifo

HOW TO WEAR

To look well in a uniform
uniform be kept in good co
pressed. See that the skirt is the rig
height and build, that the belt is adjus
that your shoes and stockings are in keeping with the
uniform, that you watch your posture and carry yourself
with dignity and grace. If the beret is removed indoors,
be sure that your hair is neat and kept in place with an
insconspicuous clip or ribbon. When you wear a
Lumberjane uniform you are identified as a member of
this organization and you should be doubly careful to
conduct yourself in a way that will show everyone that
courtesy and thoughtfullness are part of being a
Lumberjane. People are likely to judge a whole nation by
the selfishness of a few individuals, to criticize a whole
family because of the misconduct of one member, and to
feel unkindly toward and organization because of the

The unifor
helps to cre
in a group.
active life th
another bond
future, and pr
in order to b
Lumberjane pr
Penniquiqul Thi
Types, but m
can either bu
materials available at the trading post.

**AAAAND...
ADVENTURE AWAITS!**

LUMBERJANES FIELD MANUAL
CHAPTER EIGHTEEN

Lumberjanes "Literature" Program Field

DRESSIN' FOR SUCCESSIN' BADGE

"Plaid is a good way to go, always."

As a modern Lumberjane, you will be facing new and intriguing things out in the world outside of camp that we can only imagine as we put together this workbook. Time constantly changes, new trials and tribulations will face every Lumberjane, and at the same time, things don't always change. One of the concerns a Lumberjane will have in their day-to-day life from camp and even in the world beyond the camp, is how to represent themselves.

The *Dressin' for Successin'* badge is a point of pride for any Lumberjane, as they learn the importance of not only a functional wardrobe, but how to use every layer to the best of their ability. Does that sweater vest match with the preselected stockings that you brought to camp for a free day with your friends? Can it also serve as a rope and hold the weight of you and your cabin as you decide to climb the neverending tree? Perfect. Clothing looks nice, and there is nothing wrong with wanting to look nice. The best

thing that we can ever teach you at this camp is to be able to dress like you want to dress, and at the end of the day, if bracelets also work as a projectile weapon, then even better.

To obtain the *Dressin' for Successin'* badge a Lumberjane must be able to put together three outfits for a hike through the night. They will come across multiple terrains that cannot be prepared for as the terrains like to move whenever they feel like it and it will be up to the Lumberjane to put together the perfect collection of clothing to help them through any possibility. The only advice that we give our young campers as they prepare to earn this badge would be to dress comfortably, and always know that plaid has never let us down. Once you've obtained the *Dressin' for Successin'* badge, then you'll be able to move on to the next badge with relative ease, depending on your foot wear choice of the day. Keep in mind, friends are always available to help you out when it comes to this badge.

Your vest?

I like your earrings!

It is a SERIOUSLY awesome vest. Are those...

...BAND PATCHES?

Yeah, actually. I used to be in a band.

REALLY?!

Yeah, uh...in the old days...before--

Harlow?

This...

...was a mistake.

Just a mistake.

One I won't make again. Don't worry...

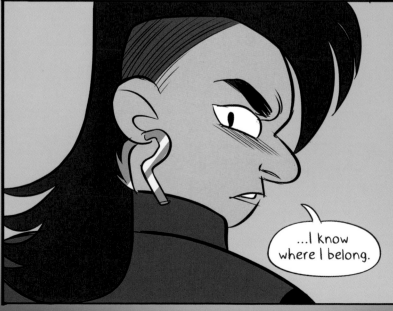

...I know where I belong.

See you around, Taylor.

Soon.

...and that's when I heard you calling me. I came over to find those serpents hounding you.

Believe me, they're PRACTICALLY harmless.

I'm sorry you had to see that back there. That gang and I...we have a lot of history.

But that's why we're here! We want to know... what happened between you all?

But, like...quickly.

Whatever happened, we want to help!

Ha, it's the oldest story in the book, isn't it?

will co

The

It hel

appearan

dress fo

Further

Lumber

to have

part in

Thiskv

Hardc

have

them

THE UNIFORM

should be worn at camp events when Lumberjanes n may also be worn at other ions. It should be worn as a the uniform dress with rect shoes, and stocking or out grows her uniform or ng ter Lumberjane. a she has her her

The yellow, short sl emb the w choose slacks, made o out-of-dc green bere the colla Shoes ma heels, rou socks shou with the shoes or wi the uniform. Ne es, bracelets, or other jewelry do belong with a Lumberjane uniform.

HOW TO WEAR THE UNIFOR

To look well in a uniform dema uniform be kept in good condit pressed. See that the skirt is the right height and build, that the belt is adjus that your shoes and stockings are in k uniform, that you watch your posture and with dignity and grace. If the beret is remo rs, be sure that your hair is neat and kept in pla with an insconspicuous clip or ribbon. When you wear a Lumberjane uniform you are identified as a member of this organization and you should be doubly careful to conduct yourself in a way that will show everyone that courtesy and thoughtfullness are part of being a Lumberjane. People are likely to judge a whole nation by the selfishness of a few individuals, to criticize a whole family because of the misconduct of one member, and to feel unkindly toward and organization because of the

The unifor helps to cre in a group. active life th another bond future, and pr in order to b Lumberjane pr Penniquiqul Thi Types, but m es will wish to have one. They can either bu w uniforms, or make it themselves from materials available at the trading post.

LUMBERJANES FIELD MANUAL

CHAPTER NINETEEN

Lumberjanes "Cooking" Program Field

ENSEMBLE ASSEMBLE! BADGE

"Some instructions may be required."

While music is an important subject that should have more focus in schools, a Lumberjane will learn the commonplace use of music in everyday situations, as well as not so everyday, from knowing the proper tone need to help your fellow camp mate out with their song to knowing the proper pitch needed in order to get everyone's attention. A Lumberjane recognizes how basic understanding of music can not only help their understanding of the flow of the world around them but how furthering that knowledge can also lead to a really good time. The human experience can be boiled down to patterns and it is with this understanding that a Lumberjane sees their importance not only in the lives that she directly influences but those outside her known friend group.

To obtain the *Ensemble Assemble!* badge, a Lumberjane must be able to play an instrument. Not only that, a Lumberjanes must be able to gather a group of their fellow campers together to form their own band in order to create unique musical treats as a group. A focus of camp is and will always be the power of friendship and teamwork and this badge is no different. The goal of this badge is to take a variety of campers at different levels in their musical growth and get them to work together to help each other grow while at the same time learning to work in tandem to create a unique sound just for that group.

With an *Ensemble Assemble!* badge, a Lumberjane will be able to read and write music. They will be able to have the basic knowledge of keys and notes, as well as how to handle an instrument of their choosing. More advanced scouts will be allowed to bring their instrument from home and use their knowledge to help their campmates earn this badge. Every cabin will be asked to play one song at the mid-camp festival every term, and each cabin will be judged by their peers. The winning cabin will receive the badge as well as a lesson from the Scout Master.

SNATCH

VOLUNTEER

VOLUNTEER

Ooof!

Jen?

Yeah Ripley?

April wouldn't make us miss the Bandicoot Bacchanal, would she?

She might.

Sometimes April gets something in her head so intensely she gets blind to what other people need.

She thinks she's doing the right thing, but she doesn't get that she's being a little selfish, too.

April wouldn't do it on purpose, Ripley.

We'll get you there...

...even if I have to jump into the water and carry her away from this ridiculous festival myself.

will co...

The...
It hel...
appearan...
dress fo...
Further...
Lumber...
to have...
part in...
Thiskv...
Hardc...
have...
them...

...E UNIFORM

...should be worn at camp ...vents when Lumberjanes ...n may also be worn at other ...ions. It should be worn as a ...the uniform dress with ...rrect shoes, and stocking or

...out grows her uniform or ...ng ...ter Lumberjane. ...a she has ...her ...f her

The...
yellow, short sl...
emb...
the w...
choose...
slacks,...
made o...
out-of-do...
green bere...
the colla...
Shoes ma...
heels, rou...
socks sho... ...th the shoes or wi...
the uniform. Ne... ...es, bracelets, or other jewelry do...
belong with a Lumberjane uniform.

...GES

HOW TO WEAR THE U...

To look well in a uniform dema...
uniform be kept in good condi...
pressed. See that the skirt is the righ...
height and build, that the belt is adj...
that your shoes and stockings are in...
uniform, that you watch your posture and...
with dignity and grace. If the beret is removed...
be sure that your hair is neat and kept in place with an
insconspicuous clip or ribbon. When you wear a
Lumberjane uniform you are identified as a member of
this organization and you should be doubly careful to
conduct yourself in a way that will show everyone that
courtesy and thoughtfullness are part of being a
Lumberjane. People are likely to judge a whole nation by
the selfishness of a few individuals, to criticize a whole
family because of the misconduct of one member, and to
feel unkindly toward and organization because of the

...helps to cre...
in a group. ...
active life th...
another bond...
future, and pr...
in order to b...
Lumberjane pr...
Penniquiqul Thi... ...ore Lady
Types, but m... ...es will wish to have one. They
can either b... ...uniform, or make it themselves from
materials available at the trading post.

LUMBERJANES FIELD MANUAL

CHAPTER TWENTY

Lumberjanes "Automotive" Program Field

KEEPIN' IT REEL BADGE

"There is more to life than fish, most of the time."

Fishing, hunting, gathering, all those good things that will be touched on in the basic survival classes are great things to know. At this camp we want to ensure that each and every Lumberjane leaves this camp with a basic understanding of what to do in a blizzard, how to survive in the desert, and what actions are needed with the ring of fire finally activates. We are happy to say that every Lumberjane that comes to this camp will leave with that knowledge and more. But knowledge and skills aren't the only things we want Lumberjanes to leave this camp with, we want Lumberjanes to have a better understand of themselves when they do eventually leave the wooden walls of their lodges.

There are a lot of distractions in the world outside of camp, and some of those distractions will follow every camper here, but to the best of our abilities we want to ensure that this camp is always a safe and welcoming environment for every camp who walks these dirt trails. At camp it is important to understand teamwork and friendship but more importantly, it is vital that you learn acceptance for who you are as a camper and gain a better understanding of that means to you. With the *Keepin' It Reel* badge, each camper is encouraged to be themselves, to find and realize that individuality they have that makes them who they are.

To obtain the *Keepin' It Reel* badge, a Lumberjane must learn the art of meditation and focus. As this is a precursor to many of the badges that need to be earned at this camp, by the time a Lumberjane is ready for the *Keepin' It Reel* badge, meditation is the least of their worries. The Lumberjane, once ready, will then figure out what they need in order to complete this badge by wandering around the camp. They will know what the object is as soon as they come across, remember this badge is all about gut instincts and not actual methods.

But...how can you say that? I saw how you and Taylor were when you were together! Jo and I sometimes fight, but then we become EVEN AWESOMER FRIENDS.

"But if neither of you are willing to bend, then...well...

SIGH

But, um, we DO need to do something about all this.

Right. Back to that.

There might not even be anything we CAN do. I mean, this concert never had a HUGE following, but whatever audience we may have had before...

...they've certainly fled by now.

GASP!

Guys guys guys guys guys **GUUUYS!**

Dang, nice slide.

I...I screwed up. Badly. I know that. I was...I was being selfish.

I saw a perfect and stupendous merhuman and I lost my head and... and...

And I wasn't a very good friend to any of you.

Ripley, I'm sorry if I ruined your dress. I know how excited you were for it.

And guys, I know it hasn't been easy teaching Bubbles how to dance.

And you, Bubbles, you really gave it your all.

SWIIIIISH

ONE!

TWO!

THREE!

FOUR!

COVER GALLERY

Lumberjanes "Wildlife" Program Field

DO THE WRITE THING BADGE

"The is pen might be mightier than the sword, but steel still hurts."

Words are a powerful tool that every Lumberjane scout will have to familiarize herself with. They carry weight, they explain things that actions can barely surmise and they open communication even during the hardest of times. Tone, nuance, and specific wording are all important no matter what language is being used. Lumberjanes will earn their *Do the Write Thing* badge as they fulfill several tasks during their time at camp. These projects will be supervised by the resident wordsmith and it will be up to that counselor to determine if a task is truly finished.

Writing is something that, while it has it's basic rules, everyone will have their own personal style for. Some Lumberjanes embrace the world of fantasy, building detailed worlds that have their own words and understanding of what it means to be have a role in the world. Others stick to the fact, they have the information that they've collected in their years and will put those facts to the page. There will be Lumberjane scouts who will be a little bit of both, and others who will push the envelope and discover that they are something else altogether.

To obtain the *Do the Write Thing* badge a Lumberjane must use her words, her passion for the world around her to create something new. It has to be something that will challenge her fellow scouts as well as push the reader in a positive direction. They need to find the words that inspire. The importance of this badge to recognize the power that words can carry, to know the feelings they can cause and the actions that will occur because of them. Words are not meant to be hidden, they are meant to be read, spoken, and shouted across the camp but every young lady at this camp will be prepare for the consequences if the words are used incorrectly.

Issue Thirteen
BROOKE ALLEN

Issue Thirteen Variant
JOY ANG

Issue Eighteen
CAROLYN NOWAK

Issue Eighteen Variant
LAUREN DAWSON

Issue Eighteen CAB Comics Exclusive
RACHEL DUKES

Issue Nineteen
CAROLYN NOWAK

Issue Nineteen Variant
MAARTA LAIHO

Issue Twenty
CAROLYN NOWAK